it was
in the stars

a sojourn in new mexico

stories and poems
by alan abrams

Sligo Creek Publishing Company
Silver Spring, Maryland

Cover Photo by Karen Thomas

Printed in the United States of America

ISBN: 979-8-9911983-0-1

First Edition

Sligo Creek Publishing Company
Silver Spring, Maryland
sligocreekpublishing.com

"...man is a dream, thought an illusion,
and only rock is real. Rock and sun."
~Edward Abbey, *Desert Solitaire*

for MAD

it was

in the stars

a sojourn in new mexico

Acknowledgments

The Black Boot[1], "Last Trip"
The Hare's Paw Literary Journal, "Crackers"
El Portal Literary Journal, "Somewhere North of Ojo Sarco"
Litbop, "Evening in Los Luceros"
The Mid Atlantic Review, "Bashō Walks"
The Winged Penny Review, "It Was in the Stars"
Frontispiece photo by Lynne Motley
Special thanks to Ricky Ray for permission to use his photo on Page 1

---

[1] Sadly, *The Black Boot* is no longer afoot

Contents

Sweat Soaked Dreams

In sweat-soaked dreams, I return
to a sun-bleached stretch of asphalt,
somewhere north of Ojo Sarco. There—
at the bottom of a barren gorge—
a silent Chevy pickup rusts away.
I, too, hold some secrets
I will carry to my grave.

photo by Ricky Ray

Last Trip

It was the big brown nose, and demonic, toothy grin that I recall most vividly. The eyes were concealed behind leatherbound goggles, and the entire assemblage capped by a half-shell helmet. He was easing past me on a BSA twin, a Lightning, I would guess.

We were already rolling along at a pretty good clip, somewhere west of Glorieta. The acid was starting to wear off, but I was still high. I glanced over at him, and nodding a greeting, goosed the throttle.

||
== O ==
||

Coming from the east coast, the landscape still seemed bleak. The high desert is reluctant to share its sparse beauty with newcomers. Annamarie was helping that process along with this ride.

She had gone out there a year or so earlier, solo, on a sweet little Honda four-banger. Rented a flat on Galisteo Street, just below the Paseo. Got a job at the Harley shop. I stopped off to visit on my way to Alaska, as I told myself.

Quickly, things got too comfortable. Within a day or two of arriving—broke—I got a job at Boddy's Honda, turning wrenches. Clarence, the shop foreman, was skeptical of my ability—maybe because when he asked my name, I told him my old friends called me Gonzo. So first morning on the job, Clarence gave me a new CB750.

"Something is wrong with the transmission. Can you open it up and fix it?"

"Sure," I replied. In Honda school, you had to tear down a transmission and reassemble it, without peeking at the manual. But it's really not hard, once you learn the system. All Honda gear boxes—large and small—share the same logical and intuitive configuration.

"OK. Let me know if you need a hand."

All I had to work with was the set of hand tools I carried in my saddlebags, but by lunchtime I had yanked the engine, split the cases, and inspected the transmission. However, there was nothing wrong with it—it was in perfect shape: shifters, dogs, gears, shafts—all sleek and gleaming. So I poked around, and found the problem: the shift linkage was fouled. A tweak with some channel locks and it was back in the groove—there had never been any need to

2

pull the engine. By late afternoon, I had the engine back in the frame, and was hooking back up the last of the cables when Clarence walked by my bay.

"Need a hand getting the engine out?"

"Nope. It's back in. I'm going for a test ride in a few minutes."

"What about the transmission?"

"It's fine. The clevis from the shift lever was bent. I straightened it. Sorry I didn't find it until I had it all torn down."

"No kidding—you had that engine apart and back together in one day— the flat rate manual gives it 24 hours! Who helped you lift the engine out?"

"Nobody."

I demonstrated how you sit astride the saddle, lay forward with your chest on the gas tank, and ease the engine up onto one of the frame tubes. You dismount, balancing the engine with one hand, then squat beside the bike, and roll the engine onto your haunches. Then you hump it onto the bench.

"Well," said Clarence, "if you want to go by Gonzo, you're Gonzo, alright. If you want to call yourself Jesus, you're Jesus."

It's no big deal, really. I worked with some serious flat-raters in shops back east, guys who were faster than me.

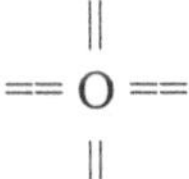

That weekend Annamarie wanted to show me one of her favorite spots. We loaded the bikes with a small tent, sleeping bags, and some food and water, and set out for the Pecos Wilderness.

In my pocket, I had a couple of squares of windowpane, powerful stuff. I had tried a dose, back in Takoma Park, just before I left. I went for a walk along the creek, and the acid came on with the rush of a jet engine. Nearing the road, the sound of the passing cars took form, growing as the car approached, and dissolving from sight as the sound receded. I walked up a hill, along a little street I never knew existed. Some old bungalows backed up to the park. As I walked beside them, one of the bungalows, low slung, with wide-eaved hip roof, transformed itself into a merry, portly woman, who hitched up her long skirts and danced a jig for me. I was eager to share this stuff with Annamarie.

We must have camped above the tree line, because I remember taking off my boots and all my clothes, and running through a meadow, and down a hill. The sun at that elevation was dazzling, and as the acid came on, clouds, mountaintops and trees took on new forms, merged, and recombined. I felt scree and thistles cutting my feet but did not perceive it as pain. It was like I was shaking off the demons of the past.

But Annamarie held back. Maybe she was worried that I would leap off some crag and try to fly away, or some local might see us and freak out and shoot us, so I chilled out. Although she was always more adventurous than me, she was a lot more circumspect. Plus, she knew I had no common sense.

I started to pull ahead of Brown Nose, and he gunned his machine in response. We were heading up a long incline, and my mildly tweaked R-60/2 was pulling him all the way. But after we crested the hill, the BSA overtook me. I had to watch it anyway, because the Beemer got a little wobbly over 95.

And so it went, I'd pace him up the hills, and he'd gain it all back going down. Soon, I could no longer see Annamarie's 350 in my mirrors. Brown Nose was in the lead when he peeled off onto the two-lane spur into Santa Fe, and I had to yield to a couple of cars. Trying to catch up, I roared up the shoulder, slinging gravel and passing traffic like crazy until a bridge abutment blocked my path. Never caught back up. It was over.

I killed the engine and waited for what seemed an hour for Annamarie to catch up. When she did, she wasn't so much angry as disgusted.

"Annamarie" on her CB350-4, somewhere in the Pecos Wilderness
(photo from the author's collection)

4

The author on his "mildly tweaked" R-60/2, late winter 1974
photo by Barbara Jacobs

I suppose it was a good thing, though, because then and there I decided that I had experienced all I needed of the psychedelic state, at least for the time. In the forty odd years since that journey to the Pecos, I've never dropped another hit. Even tapered off of *mota*, and finally quit that, too.

But I reserve the right to try it again some time. Like if I were diagnosed with terminal cancer, maybe. Or if Brown Nose blasted out of the hills again, to give me another chance.

Crackers

Crackers was a dog who never knew a leash. I'll get to his finer qualities, but first—I must admit that I am not a dog person. And I'm really not a puppy person. I don't like their smell, and I particularly don't like discovering their turds in my bare feet.

You may think it was Cracker's misfortune, to come to be raised by me, to be barricaded at night into a corner of the bathroom, but I was the one who had to listen to him squeal.

Man, he could piss me off. Like that time I walked into the trailer house and smelled something.

"What's that smell?" I demanded.

Annamarie was sitting across the room reading a book. Crackers was by her feet, stretched out with his head on his front paws.

"What smell?" she replied.

"Like something died in here."

"I don't smell anything."

Crackers lifted his head and sniffed the air.

"Over here somewhere."

Annamarie came over and she smelled it too. The dog came over and sniffed around our feet. We looked around, but didn't see anything, so I started searching. Down the hall, into the nook, into the bathroom, the closet. Nothing. Into the bedroom. Nothing. Under the bed. Nothing. I tromped back down the hall, baffled. The smell seemed worse now.

"Maybe something died under the trailer," she suggested. So I grabbed a flashlight and went outside. Crackers trotted after me.

I searched under the trailer but could not find anything obvious. But I still smelled something.

Still baffled, I headed back to the door. There I saw it—the unidentifiable remains of some unfortunate critter, delivered by Crackers, and smooshed into the doormat by a Vibram soled boot. The boot print, which matched my own size thirteen, was pointed toward the door.

I sat down on the edge of the stoop and lifted my ankle up onto my knee, and twisted my foot up so I could see the sole. More of the remains were embedded in the lugs, and I could see carpet fibers embedded in the glistening tissue. Crackers came over to sniff.

"Shit!" I hollered. "Goddam you," I screamed, whipping off the boot. "You stupid animal," I bellowed, as the boot chased the dog across the driveway.

But the boot could not catch up with the dog, so it gave up the chase and tumbled into the arroyo. The dog just stood there by the fence, looking at me quizzically.

Crackers, however, had a generous heart. He forgave me for throwing the boot, like he forgave me for penning him in the bathroom.

||
== O ==
||

Crackers was really Annamarie's companion. He'd give me that low growl when I came on to her. Still, we got along fine. Me, throwing a tennis ball, sidearm, just as hard as I could, skimming it down the dirt road. Crackers would tear after it, his paws sending up rooster tails of dust and gravel, until he reached full speed. He'd gallop back with the ball, nearly as fast, like Pete Rose sprinting up the first base line on a walk, proud of his powerful legs.

Then I'd fling the ball again, way into the brush. Crackers would search relentlessly, never returning without it, never not eager to go after it again. An hour would pass, just like that.

He was a mutt we picked up at the pound. We got him after we were burglarized, back when we lived on Galisteo Street, in Santa Fe.

I knew who did it, too. It was this skinhead who used to hang around the neighborhood. Don't ask me to remember his name. He noticed our motorcycles parked behind the wall that formed the miniature courtyard in front of the flat and struck up a conversation with me. He was wearing a gun on his hip, like some fetish object. "It's legal, you know, as long as it's not concealed."

One evening he knocked on the door and I let him in. He made a feeble effort to make conversation, asking dumb questions about motorcycles. But he just sort of gazed around the room, not listening to the answers.

The next evening, we came home and I noticed that a block had been knocked loose from the wall out front. Strange. Inside, it took a moment to discover the guitar was missing. Damn! Just an old gut string no-name. But still. Oh my god—where's my tool chest? It contained a complete collection of Snap-on wrenches and sockets, large and small air wrenches, special tools for Beemers, and some custom tools I had made or modified. It took a day or two to miss the Yashica rangefinder my brother had given me.

So we went to the pound and selected a pup that looked like it might be a German shepherd. He got his name from a dysfunctional character in a John Waters movie. Just for good measure, I bought a gun. Then we moved out of town.

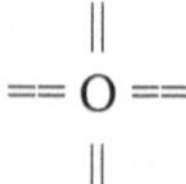

Crackers grew to be a formidable dog. He looked like a shepherd collie mix: shaggy coat, black, tan, and white, a husky trunk. But his legs were unusually short. You might say, like a Corgi--but he was twice as large. As odd as he looked, I saw many similar dogs running around the countryside.

Regardless of his lineage, the short strong legs stood him in good stead. We'd go for jaunts in the high desert, and when we'd come to the edge of a steep barranca, I'd pick him up—all forty-five pounds of him—and fling him over the brink. Then I'd leap after him, half free falling, half trotting down the slope, just touching the ground whenever it approached, a quick little double step, tipTAP, tipTAP, not knowing where I was going, or where I would land, letting my feet decide all that. Somehow, we'd always arrive at the bottom, together, upright.

I remember pausing at the rim of a broad, deep arroyo, watching some canyon jays on the opposite side. They were flying around erratically, calling out in crow-like squawks, but in a higher pitch. Just then, I remembered a bird call I had in my wallet. A girl from back east had given me a duck call, a total riff. I had stuffed it in my wallet and forgotten about it.

I sat down on the rim and unwrapped the package. Crackers sat on his haunches beside me as I read the directions. Then I put it up to my mouth and blew. The duck call must have meant something to the jays, because one of them immediately flew over to scope things out. Then a few more flew over. They were calling like mad, and I was calling back, trying to imitate their pitch and intonations. More and more of them came from out of nowhere, and soon there were countless birds, swirling and darting over us and around us. Crackers would follow the flight of one, and then another, wishing he had wings so he could join them. Soon the birds got tired of the game, and one by one, went back about their business.

We slept out in the open that night, under the stars. Whenever I camped out, I was haunted by that scene from Easy Rider, where some thugs club the Jack Nicholson character to death. You could hike way back into the wilderness, imagining no one had ever passed that way before, but no matter where you went, you'd look down and see an empty Coors can or a spent rifle shell. Before I went to sleep, I tied a thong around my wrist, with the other end tied around the revolver's trigger guard. It was comforting to feel the warmth from the dog next to me.

His stirring woke me in the middle of the night. The milky way sprung up out of the mountains beyond and ranged over our bodies. In the distance, a pack of coyotes was singing.

I reached over and grabbed the loose flesh behind his ear and kneaded it firmly. He hunkered back down and closed his eyes.

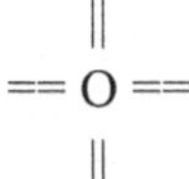

It's been a while since I heard a coyote sing, but I still can hear a feral call in the distance from time to time. It used to be—with any pinch or a tug from my own leash—always one I would wriggle into voluntarily, eagerly—I would heed the call and slip the noose, leaping off the edge with no clue, no care, of what the next step would be. But somehow those journeys have taken me to a place where I am content, happy to listen to the call without giving chase.

An Excerpt from *The Journeys of Jack Isaksen*

Chapter 6: The Beauty of a Woman

…as the two continued east, Jack's misgivings receded. They bent to the northeast at Deming and picked up the main highway at Hatch. For two hundred miles, they traveled along the Rio Grande valley and its narrow band of irrigated orchards and fields. Jack, with a gas station road map, ticked off the little villages along the way. The inscrutably named Truth or Consequences, Socorro, Belen. As they approached Albuquerque, the Sandia Mountains loomed to the east. He was surprised when Gizmo turned west at Bernalillo.

"I have to take you through some country that will blow your mind," said Gizmo. "It's not like we're in any kind of hurry, anyway."

At San Ysidro, Gizmo turned again, this time onto a lonely two-lane road with no shoulders. They followed a bouldered canyon, along a stream lined with cottonwoods. The road cut through a Pueblo settlement—a school, a convenience store, a scattering of small adobe-walled homes with corrugated metal roofs. Continuing upstream, past some orchards and gardens, evidence of human habitation thinned out, and the sides of the valley grew steeper.

Here, Gizmo slowed down and peered carefully at the right side of the road. At last, he cried out, "Here it is!"

Jack said, "What is it?"

"You'll see." Gizmo pulled off the road and drove a short distance down an unpaved lane. They reached a small, cleared open area, where a Dodge Dart was parked. Gizmo pulled in beside it, turned off the engine, and got out of the truck. Mystified, Jack followed him out.

Gizmo looked over the Dart and noticed a University of New Mexico parking sticker on the rear bumper. On the other side of the bumper was a peeling sticker that read, NIX ON NIXON.

"Let's see who's here," said Gizmo. "I feel the presence of *chicitas.*"

Here we go again, thought Jack, as Gizmo walked down a narrow path, past fragrant junipers and piñons. Just beyond they saw a pool that was nothing more than a hot spring captured by some crudely arranged rocks and boulders. Three young women lay half submerged in the steaming pool. Their clothing and towels lay in neat piles on a large boulder.

Gizmo put out his arm to stop Jack. Together they gazed at the unsuspecting naiads. Two of them were lithe and fair skinned: one, a blonde; the other, a redhead. The third woman had thick, jet-black hair, and skin the hue of a cured tobacco leaf, smooth and taut. They were enjoying an animated conversation until Jack shifted his weight, his boot dislodging some scree.

As the pebbles cascaded down into the pool, the two light-skinned women shrieked and clutched for their towels. Gizmo laughed and bellowed, "Don't worry, *mis bellezas*, we won't bite you." He and Jack glimpsed bits of pale flesh not meant to be seen in daylight as the two fairer ones got out of the pool and wrapped themselves up.

The author with two *bellezas*, in Santa Fe, May 1974
photo by Eddie McMullen

The third woman remained serene, leaning back against a boulder with only her legs submerged. *"Ola, señors,"* she said.

The other two women had gathered their clothes and scurried behind a clump of piñons to dress. The blonde called to the one in the pool, "Marcella, we better get going. Jill has to get to work."

"I'm coming," said Marcella. She stood up to gather her clothing without any attempt to conceal herself. She was short; little in the way of contour between her shoulders and her legs. Her jaw was heavy, her cheeks full, and her eyes were large and close-set. Gizmo conversed with her in Spanish, telling her his name, and then adding something Jack couldn't understand. Her replies were spoken so rapidly that Jack could only pick out a few words, UNM, *escuela de Medicina, últimosemestre,* and *Pueblo de San Juan.*

She finished dressing, walked up the slope toward the path, and handed Gizmo a ballpoint pen. She recited a phone number, which Gizmo wrote down on his forearm. The other two women, now dressed, caught up with Marcella, giggling as they passed the two men.

When they had gone, Gizmo said to Jack, "That was the most beautiful woman I ever saw."

Jack said, "Which one, the blonde or the redhead? Either one could have been a movie star."

Gizmo replied, "No, man, the other one."

Jack looked at him, confused. He said, "Ha! You mean the runt of the litter? C'mon, get serious."

Gizmo shook his head. "*Gringo,* in all the time I have known you, I seem to have taught you nothing about women. I feel like I've let you down. Yes, those other two were hot all right. But that's all on the surface. Marcella is beautiful without any of that—the big hair, the perfect tits, all that Playboy shit. Marcella, she has pride, and I don't mean like sinful pride. She wasn't ashamed of anything, her body, her face. She was not ashamed to stand naked in front of a man. That's real beauty. Powerful beauty. Dammit, she is so beautiful I want to cry. It's not even like I want to fuck her. I mean I would, in a heartbeat. But that's not the point. Anyway, we might be cousins."

"How's that?" asked Jack.

"She grew up in San Juan Pueblo. That's just a few miles south of my home. My father's father came from there, too. So, you never know."

"Hey, let's get back to the truck. For all we know, your girl Marcella grabbed the coke, and made off to Albuquerque on my bike."

"Fat chance, but you're right. We don't want to tempt an honest woman to go bad . . ."

Bashō Walks

"I might as well be going to the ends of the earth"!
~Matsuo Bashō

Proudly the land wears its poverty. Once self-sufficient farms, subdivided among sons, resubdivided among grandsons: plots grown narrower, shallower, great grandson's well down the slope from grandson's septic field. Pickup trucks with rifle racks, a little white cross festooned with plastic flowers at every sharp bend in the road. Summer, clouds of mosquitos; winter, haze of piñon smoke. In the few remaining orchards, peach and apple blossoms grace spring's arrival.

All this bounded by mountains: to west, the Jemez; Sandia to the south. Along the easterly horizon range the mighty Sangre de Cristos, where vestiges of snow linger through Leo.

I sojourned here, in the valley of the Rio Grande, working with my hands, living in a rented trailer house barely 8 feet wide. Halos of frost on the bedroom wall where our heads had lain. Kicking my frigid bike to life at five degrees above, then riding 40 miles to work. And somewhere, way out there beyond Redondo Peak, the hippy haven hot spring. Fifty years later I sought it out.

this two-lane highway
mountains tell it where to bend
where to rise and fall

I crept

along the road to San Ysidro, searching for the unpaved turnoff. I remembered it was somewhere past the Jemez Pueblo, in a steep bouldered canyon. Along the way,

> *I pause among pines*
> *overwhelmed by their silence*
> *then the wind rises*

I did not find what I was looking for, thus continued on my journey. The next day, approaching Denver,

> *the landscape dissolves*
> *tall signs—gas—food—sad to be*
> *back in the city*

A journey cluttered with memories—perhaps more real than the moment itself. I mourned my foolish choices, blown opportunities, my abandoned lover. My consolation is my pen, however humble the words that flow from it.

> *Bashō walks; I drive*
> *no wonder my poor words*
> *pale before the Master*

Chapter 7: The *Brujo*

Florio's woman was out front, splitting bolts of pine. Her strokes were rhythmic; one lick was all it took to lop off a slab the size of a 2x6. As she raised the ax to take another bite, she caught a glimpse of a truck struggling up the steep rutted road, still a quarter mile away. She slammed the ax into the chopping block and went into the house to report this to her man. He was still abed, but he had already heard the grinding engine and crunching gravel. The woman asked him, "Do you want me to bring you the gun?"

The old man replied, "No. What do we have that anyone would want to steal?" Still barefoot and in his boxers, he rose and joined the woman out on the shallow, covered porch. There, they observed the unannounced guests, as their truck weaved among towering Ponderosas, and bucked over the washouts.

Florio Martinez, the brother of Gizmo's mother, hinted at what Gizmo would have looked like, were he to live another 35 years. Although his paunch hung precipitously over his waistband, he was otherwise wiry, with knotted forearms, and a posture that had only begun to hunch. Gray had nearly overtaken the black in his thick hair and bushy mustache. He had a multitude of creases in his forehead and cheeks, but the flesh was still firm. When he bared his teeth to smile, which seemed to be his natural disposition, they were remarkably white, which accentuated the upper incisor that was replaced with gold. The only thing to interrupt the symmetry of his face was a patch that concealed the empty eye socket, the contents lost somewhere in Belgium, during the early winter of 1944.

The truck finally arrived, and the two young men got out. Gizmo hollered, "*Tío Florio, soy yo, Guillermo!*"

"*Ah, Gizmo, es tan bueno verte,*" cried Florio. Gizmo grabbed his right hand with both of his own, and then embraced his uncle. Florio pointed to the Dodge and said, "Nice truck, Gizmo. Things must be going well for you. Is that your motorcycle, too?"

Gizmo replied, "No, Tio, the bike belongs to my friend. But things are going very well. It's good to be alive–and to be free."

"I must agree with you. And it seems the older I get, the freer I feel."

"Are you saying that you wish to be free of me?" asked the old woman.

"No, Anita, not until you prepare some refreshments for our guests."

Anita turned to Gizmo and said, for his benefit and Florio's, "He forgets how cold his feet get at night."

"Bah!" said Florio. "I could get a dog, you know."

Anita replied, "There is already a dog in your bed, and it is not me." Then she went inside.

Then Florio said, "Gizmo, you have not introduced me to your friend."

Gizmo said in English, "This is Jack. I have been trying to teach him good Spanish for…how many years now?

Jack replied, in halting Spanish, "Senor, we have been friends for five years. I apologize for my poor Spanish. It's not Gizmo's fault."

In perfect English, Florio said, "I'm very pleased to meet you, Jack. But Anita is right, I do get cold more easily these days. And right now, the wind is whistling around my *cojones*. Let's go inside."

Jack had to duck under the lintel. Inside, he paused to take in the space. The walls were coated with a sandy material, nearly white, that undulated over the adobe bricks beneath. Where daylight penetrated, the walls had a luminous quality. The floor was set with rugged flagstones, random shapes, the tawny pink colors of the barrancas. One thin carpet woven in a geometric pattern was centered in the room. The ceiling was framed with pine logs, crudely stripped of their bark with a drawknife. Pine planks, wide and narrow, spanned over the logs. All the wood had oxidized with age, turning it to warm golds and browns. Though the space was dim, all the surfaces seemed to radiate warmth.

At the opposite end was the kitchen, little more than a dry sink and a shelf along the outer wall. A wood fired cook stove stood alone near the center of the space. Off to one corner was a table and two mismatched chairs. On the adjacent wall hung a large bear hide. Another two chairs and a low table sat along the south wall of the house. A chess set, with a game in progress, was set up on the table. Adjacent to this was a pair of casement windows. A huge tuxedo cat slept on the deep sill in a splash of sunlight. Opposite this, in the recess of the el, was a double bed covered in handmade quilts. A few kerosene lamps were scattered about. Two crudely carved cottonwood santos—one of the Virgin and Child, and another of St. Francis, stood on either side of the door.

The three men walked in first. Florio grabbed a third chair and placed it at the dining table. He sat with his back to the bear hide, and invited Jack and Gizmo to join him. Anita placed a few more wooden slabs into the firebox. Then she took a large jug with her outside. As the men exchanged pleasantries, they heard the clanking of the pump handle, and soon the rhythmic gush of water filling the jug.

Florio said, "The woman was nagging me to get a proper well dug. So I called the driller, and he told me I needed a permit. I went all the way up to Tierra Amarilla, and I show the guy where we want to drill on his map. He tells me, 'You're not in Rio Arriba County, you're in Taos County. So I go up to Taos, and they tell me the people in TA are full of shit, that this is in Rio Arriba. Then I hire a surveyor. He comes out with two guys and their instruments and they run around here for two days. Cost me six hundred bucks. Know what he told me? I'm in the fucking Carson National Forest, and they don't give anybody a well permit. In fact, it means the house is illegal!

"This house, my friends, they tell me is over one hundred and fifty years old. It was here before the United States came here and took the land. And I believe this damned house will be here by the time someone else takes the land from the United States. Anyway, as long as I have the woman, I don't need a new well."

Florio did not realize that Anita had just walked in, in time to hear the last remark. After sitting the jug down, she stood over him and said, "They got it wrong, when they say you don't miss your water til the well runs dry. What they should say, is you don't miss your woman til she finds a better man."

Florio grabbed her arm and pulled her into his lap. He forced a kiss on her and said, "'Nita, why is it that the worse you are to me, the more I love you?'"

She replied, "Because you are a fool. But since all men are fools, I may as well stay with you." Then she leapt up and went back to the kitchen.

"You see," said Florio to Gizmo, "Nothing has changed up here. Nothing, except I walk slower, and everything hurts. But we get by. A few dinero from Social. A little from the VA–although I would have gotten five times as much if I had lost both eyes." Then, speaking to the woman, "It might have been worth it to lose them both, so I wouldn't have to look at you."

The woman, who had been preparing a pot of tea, brandished a spoon at him and said, "I would be only too pleased to oblige you." Then she served the men their tea, and sat down to study the chess game. The cat woke, stretched, and sat in her lap.

Then, sipping tea, and knowing better than to ask for a drink, Gizmo summarized the last few years for his uncle. His life as a fisherman, then meeting Jack, and then getting cast aside by Stella, Anita's niece by marriage. Finally, getting mixed up in the drug running business, inadvertently holding an incalculably valuable piece of contraband.

Florio listened without interruption. When Gizmo finished, Florio said to his guests, "After I dropped out of high school, I became a thief. I would hit the tourists who camped up at Hyde Park. It was so easy it was silly. I knew all the trails. I had a set of tools made from strips of sheet metal that would open any car or truck. I stole everything! Guns, rifles, fishing tackle; all kinds of expensive camping gear. I was even stealing stuff I didn't need and couldn't sell. Sometimes I would just leave the stuff on the path, because I didn't feel like carrying it home. Back then, I figured it was OK, because they were all Texans. Or maybe because they were all white."

Gizmo said, "But Tio, you're white, too."

"Yes, but not like Jack–no offense, young man. And I'm one quarter Indio, too. I knew where I stood in the world. Not accepted by the Pueblos–even with my name. Looked down on by the Anglos. It all made it easier to steal from them, like they had stolen the land.

"But then the war came. It changes you. They teach you to hate when you join the Army. It makes it easier to kill your brother. We were very good at killing. We got medals for it. But it never got easy. For some it did, but for me it just got harder. When I lost my eye, they sent me home a hero. I had a bronze star and a purple heart. I never showed them to anyone. No, as soon as I could, I threw them off the Otowi Bridge."

Gizmo said, "I never knew you won the bronze star. What did you do to earn it?"

"I don't want to talk about it."

"Please!"

"I'd like to know, too," said Jack."

"If you must. It was when we were on recon. I was driving my lieutenant way out in front of our lines when the jeep got hit. It broke both of the louie's legs. I took shrapnel in the eye, but I could see OK out of the other one. So I carried him back to our lines. It was no big deal; he was a little guy."

"Well that sure was heroic."

"No, heroism is just bullshit. All this was, was just doing what had to be done. They should ban giving medals. It just makes people hungrier for war."

Anita called from the kitchen, "Did you say you were hungry? I am making dinner right now."

"Keep your nose out of this, woman. This is man's talk."

"You mean your bragging and lying."

"Bah! Maybe so. But it beats women's carping and gossip."

Jack could not help snickering at that exchange. Gizmo turned to scowl at him. But Florio let out a laugh, too, and said, "Enough of that *basura*. Tell me about yourself, young man."

Jack looked at Gizmo, who gave him a nod. At that, Jack told his own story, emphasizing how Gizmo had taken him under his wing, effectively becoming his big brother and his mentor—at least as it pertained to romance.

When Jack finished, Florio said, "I must tell you, your eyes tell the story of your sorrow. The way you hold your shoulders tells the story of your worries. What lies at the heart of it all is the guilt you bear, for what you feel you've done wrong."

Florio paused there and looked around. The woman stood still, with dishes in her hands. Gizmo looked out the window, avoiding everyone else's eyes. Jack stared at his hands, clasped together on the table.

"But your story is not unique. Most of us break with our fathers. Not always with blows, like you and your father; sometimes, without even a word. Either that, or we remain children. And we all do foolish things, as I have explained before. These things cannot be undone. You can repair some of the damage, but like a broken teacup, you can glue it back together, but you will always see the cracks. These cracks, these scars, they must be lived with. Let us talk more about this later."

The woman resumed serving the plates to the men. She took her own meal and sat down again at the chess game, plate in her lap. The cat clawed at her knees and sniffed at the plate. But the woman was lost in concentration over her next move on the board, and the cat retreated to the bed.

Neither Gizmo nor Jack had eaten breakfast, so their plates were quickly emptied. Florio ate only a few bites and got up to put his plate on the dry sink. The cat came over and stood on its hind legs. Florio gave it his left-over meat, which the cat carried off under the bed to eat.

"You should not have fed him," said the woman. "He'll let the mice run wild in here tonight."

He turned to his guests and said, "Damn that woman. Always thinking one move ahead. No wonder she always beats me at chess."

Then he turned to Gizmo and said, "How long has it been since you've been home?"

Gizmo replied, "Six years, I think. It was after I got out of the Navy."

"You must go to them tonight. My sister misses you deeply. She says you never even write."

"That's true," said Gizmo. But I think about her all the time. Papi, too."

"It's not enough to miss someone. You must tell them…"

"Alright!" shouted Gizmo. "Goddammit, stop telling me what to do. Don't you think I know?"

"Gizmo, I apologize for making you feel uncomfortable. But you must acknowledge that you are too easy to love. It makes you forget that others need your love, too."

After barking at his uncle, Gizmo calmed himself down. He said, "I apologize, too, Tio."

"It's OK. We got that off our chests. Why don't you go now, while there's still a little light. Jack can stay here. I want to talk to him some more."

"OK, Tio. I'll get on my way. It will be too dark to return tonight, so I will see you again tomorrow."

"Good, and I will be thinking about your problem, too."

After Gizmo left, Florio told Jack to relax while he attended to some chores. He went to the stove and pulled out a piece of burning wood. Then he went out and picked up a few more pieces from what the woman had stacked. He took them up a path behind the house, climbing even further up the slope of the mountain. Around the path were patches of snow, preserved in the shade of the dense pine canopy.

At last, he reached a clearing where there was a small domed hut made of cow hides stretched over a frame of willow branches. He pulled aside one of the hides and crawled in through a small opening. He placed the burning log in a ring of stones and placed the other logs around it. He knew just how to blow on the flame to ignite the other logs. When it was all ablaze, he placed several large stones over top of the fire. He watched as the smoke drifted up through an aperture in the top of the hut.

He took his time returning to the house. Several times he stopped to listen for the owl that usually began its hunt at sundown. Then he picked up his pace. He'd not seen a bear near his home in years, but you can never be sure.

When he got back to the house, Jack was sitting across from the woman, who was teaching him how to play chess. Florio filled a large mason jar with water. Then said to Jack, "I am sorry to interrupt this lesson, but I would like you to come with me."

Jack got up and followed Florio outside. Jack followed him up the slope, amazed how the old man, out of doors, and in the darkening woods, moved like a cat, silently, stealthily. Jack had to hustle to keep up. Lagging behind, he called to Florio, Senor, where are we going? To raid some Texan campers?"

Florio looked back and hissed, "Be quiet!"

When they arrived at the hut, Florio told Jack to strip. They hung their clothing on the branches of a scrub oak, and then the two naked men entered the hut. Florio splashed some of the water on the rocks, which instantly turned to steam. Jack began to sweat profusely. Florio closed his single eye and chanted something in Tewa. Then he handed the mason jar to Jack.

"Drink it all," he said to Jack. "Then sweat it back out. Let the sweat carry away all the rubble in your brain. Let each drop of sweat carry one stone."

Florio began chanting again. Jack did not understand a word of it. He could not pick up a line that repeated itself, like in the refrain of a song. There was nothing in it that rhymed. Although Florio spoke rhythmically, there was no pattern to it. Maybe, thought Jack, he was making up the words as he went on.

His sweating began to abate, and he grew sleepy. Suddenly, Florio smacked him, hard, on the side of his face. Jack gasped and rubbed his cheek.

Florio said, "That blow was to drive away the last stone. It was delivered out of love. Now, I hope you will be able to chart your course wisely."

Florio crawled out of the hut and held the flap for Jack. He said, "Let's cool off before we dress." Then he walked over to a patch of snow and sat down in it, scooping handfuls and calmly rubbing it on his head and face, and all over his body. Jack followed suit, shuddering with every handful. When they stood, the breeze that had swept across the high desert dried them in no time. They dressed in silence and returned to the house. Florio spread a few blankets on the floor beside the still warm stove. Jack sank into a deep dreamless sleep. He woke at dawn; the stove cold, and the cat asleep on his chest…

… Now tell me how I can help you."

"Yes. I hate to bring this up," said Gizmo, "but I thought maybe you know someone who could take the—stuff—"

Florio interrupted. "You mean drugs."

"Yes, the drugs. I want to sell it, to make a home for Mami—a nice place, and maybe hire people to take care of her and Papi, and the house. They've worked so hard; they deserve some comfort."

"What makes you think I can help you sell—your drugs?"

"Naranjo."

"You mean Emilio?"

"Yes, your friend the sheriff."

"Hah! Emilio. You know he helped me get my VA disability. When I came home half blind, I was supposed to get a twenty percent disability. I filed, and nothing happened. I know it was hard for the Coloreds, but I thought Indio were OK. Maybe they thought Indios were Colored, too. Anyway, Emilio knew some people in Santa Fe. It took a year, but I got the disability, even all the money I should have gotten since my discharge."

"You know he had a reputation. That he was corrupt. That he took money."

"Oh, there's no doubt. He is powerful here. And he loves money. The Cadillac, the fancy boots, a different Stetson for every day of the week. No wonder, he grew up an orphan. But he helped me out when I needed it. He has helped many others, too. Sometimes a crooked man will do good things."

"Then will you ask him—if he knows someone?"

"Gizmo, I believe it would be better to toss that junk into the Rio. Like I did with my medals. I am worried that something evil attaches itself to these drugs. And that it can't help but attach itself to the money when it is sold."

"But you take mescaline. You take peyote."

"Yes, I took them, but neither of them enslaved me. They opened doors for me. I learned a little about what was inside my head, and a little more about what was outside it. And then I decided I knew as much as any man should know, and I quit. Cocaine is different—it makes slaves of its users. It makes the seller a slaver."

"I am not a slaver. I would never make anyone use cocaine. People use it of their own free will. I just want to make my mother happy."

"Yes, I understand, but we may have to disagree on that point. Still, I will speak with Emilio. But only for my sister's sake. I will ask him if he can help another scoundrel to do good things for his mother. Now let's go inside."

The next day the three men piled into Florio's ancient GMC and rode to Española. Gizmo tried unsuccessfully to convince his one-eyed uncle that he shouldn't be driving. Fortunately, the old truck was not capable of speed that would have made the journey hazardous. Arriving in town, they stopped at the Sheriff's office, but Emilio was not there. Florio said, "I have a hunch where to find him."

They walked around the corner, past the headquarters of the Rio Arriba County Democratic Party, of which Emilio was chairman. Then, past the next building, which housed the Naranjo Insurance Agency. Finally, they arrived at the restaurant that bore his name: Emilio's. The rear of the restaurant was comprised of booths, each elaborately decorated in a Southwestern theme. In the right corner was a teepee motif, on the left, a sort of corral. The center booth was made to look like a jail cell. In this make-believe prison sat a pudgy man with an almost spherical head. Florio told his companions to go sit at the bar and made his way to the back.

Emilio looked up from a pile of papers as the man approached. With daylight pouring in from the front of the restaurant, Florio's face was in shadow. It was not until Florio stood at the opening to the cell that Emilio recognized him, and beckoned for him to sit down.

By the time Florio returned, Gizmo and Jack had polished off three beers each, and several rounds of salsa and chips. Florio put two fives on the bar and said, "Let's go . . ."

Ode to Emilio

In every tiny village,
and nameless clot of homes,
strung along the Chama River,
and back up the Rio Grande,
he was known by his first name—*Emilio.*

They patronized the agency
where he sold insurance,
drank and dined at his restaurant,
both known by that familiar name—*Emilio.*

Mostly they admired him,
forgave his venial sins,
and voted him to office,
time and time again. Nor
did they begrudge
the modest fortune he amassed,
which he shared sometimes
with those in need,
and also his greedy friends—
that ever generous *Emilio.*

But a bantam cock is bound to make
his share of enemies,
La Raza sought to free the county
from his vise-like grip,
contesting him in court
and in the voting booth.
failing every time—
too many loved—*Emilio.*

Not even

the state could touch him,
though they harried him with gusto—
nobody ever laid a glove on Emilio *Naranjo*.

"Emilio Naranjo met with opposition at the Santa Fe County Courthouse Jan. 29, 1979, when he was sentenced following his perjury trial. District Court Judge Ray Hughes compared the Naranjo scandal to Watergate. The conviction was eventually overturned." ~Rio Grande *Sun*, 8/29/19

Something of Value

The last time I saw Pat Maloney was at the Denny's in Santa Fe. At first, I didn't recognize him, clean shaven, in a neatly pressed shirt—and without the crazy stalker hat. But yes, it was Pat, sitting across the dining room, eating dinner by himself. There was a time when we were close—but now, the last thing I wanted was to talk to him.

A year earlier, Pat had dropped out of sight, leaving me to finish out the Grant project on my own. That was bad enough, but what I heard was that he had run out on Rosa and Marcella as well. The word was that Pat had cleaned out their bank account, driven off with the Tornado, and left Rosa with that bombed out Country Squire he used for hauling around his table saw. I figured he had gone back to Great Barrington, where he would hide out for a while whenever domestic life got him down. And then return yet again, like a serial prodigal husband. That Pat was eating alone suggested that Rosa would not have him back. When I returned from the salad bar, I was glad that he was gone.

photo cadged from eBay

After turning wrenches for four years back east, and in Santa Fe for Boddy's Honda, and then the Kawasaki dealer, and finally at the Harley shop, I'd had it with the oil and grease, the brake dust and exhaust fumes, the bone deep slices in every knuckle—and most of all, the grimy stains that no soap, no solvent would wash out of my hands.

A classified ad sought carpenters in White Rock. I contacted old man Sandoval, the SnapOn dealer, and met him at his house in Arroyo Seco. I carried in a carton with two air wrenches, an air chisel, and some other specialized tools I knew I wouldn't be using again. I walked out of the house with a battered Skil Model 77, a well-worn leather tool belt, and a framing square. No money changed hands, and each of us thought he got the better of the other.

Next day, I put the tools in the bed of my truck and hauled myself across the Rio, and up the highway that scales the rugged slopes of the Pajarito Plateau. The Sandias and the Sangre de Cristos panned in and out of view as I negotiated the switchbacks. Up on the flats, a trim young jogger loped along the road that ran to Los Alamos. A fox, half hidden in the brush, watched his progress. Beyond the fox, the terrain rose to Redondo Peak.

A little way down the road, this wilderness gave way to suburbia. At first, I missed the street named in the want ad, and wound down the lane all the way to the rim of the plateau. The land fell off more than two thousand feet to the Rio. I heard a plaintive wailing, almost like a child. A thousand feet below me a string of geese were working their way south.

I probably took the longest possible route back along the coiling lanes to La Senda and found the house. It was a timber framed structure, with slump-block walls and great glass panels. Sitting on a rolling five-acre lot, surrounded by stubby piñons, its form was ranging and aggressive—a prairie style house for the high desert.

I pulled into the driveway. A carpenter was leaning precariously from a ladder, as he nailed up cedar shakes on a curved section of wall. A lean, weather-beaten man was standing nearby with a clipboard in his hand and a roll of drawings under his arm. He wore tooled leather boots with pointed toes, and a straw hat with the brim rolled up on the sides, so the front also came to a point. I got out of the truck and asked him if he knew about the job offer. With his free hand, he took the cigarette out of his mouth.

"You carpenter?"

The right answer was no. The biggest thing I'd ever made using a hammer and saw was a plywood camper shell for Annamarie's Datsun. But I was pretty good with motors and transmissions—how much harder could this be?

I glanced over at the building. Even though it was chilly, the carpenter who was nailing up the shakes had taken off his shirt. I flashed back to my college days, when I got a summer job working at the library. It was at the main branch, and my job was opening cartons of new books and gluing the envelope under the back cover. A new wing was being added to the library, and I would look out the window of the dingy storeroom and watch the guys tiptoeing across a run of open joists carrying sheets of plywood, out under the open sky.

"I'm pretty good with wood," I replied.

He peered into the truck bed. Ah see ya use a worm drive," he said, nodding at the Model 77. "Anything else is a piece a shit. Kin you start now? Ah'll give ya four-fifty."

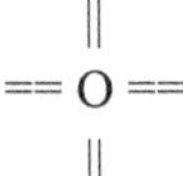

Pat Maloney was older than the rest of us. Having served a formal apprenticeship as a cabinet maker, he took a paternal interest in our work, teaching us how to sharpen a chisel or plane iron. He would test the edge by shaving the hair on his forearm. Using hand tools, he could layout and cut a mortise and tenon joint with machine-like precision, probably as fast as someone using a router and power saw. He mesmerized us with stories of living and working on a pheasant hunting resort, raising the birds, maintaining the incubators and coops, guiding the hunters. To us, it sounded like an idyllic existence.

During that time, he met Rosa, a sophomore at Amherst. When she got pregnant, she dropped out, and moved in with him for a while, in his gamekeeper's apartment above the workshop. But she left him behind to have the baby, back with her family in Santa Fe.

Pat followed her to New Mexico to marry her, but soon grew uncomfortable in what to him was an alien environment. He could not persuade Rosa to move back east, so he left her alone with an infant. Then, he began a pattern of wandering back and forth across the country, in and out of the lives of his wife and daughter. Pat was a pendulum that swung between the people and places he loved, repelled from one pole by the unbearable burdens of marriage and fatherhood, and from the other by the desperate forces of loneliness and sentiment.

Our mutual oscillations coincided in White Rock. Pat was already working on the project when I got hired, but it took a while to get to know him. For one thing, I was canned a day after I started.

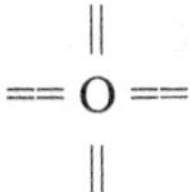

I was a disappointment to the man who assumed I was equal to my tools. That first day on the job, he assigned me to frame out for a big bathtub within the circular walls. While the shirtless carpenter pounded on the walls from the outside, I struggled to resolve the interplay of arc and rectangle. It was a task for a top notch, experienced craftsman, and by the end of the day I had maybe two ill-fitting boards nailed up.

The next day, the foreman walked in and watched me struggle for a while. "Son, yerbuildin' a house, not a pie-anner," he advised. By the end of the day, he'd let me go.

"Ain'tgonna fuss with a check, son." He pulled out his wallet and peeled off three twenties. "S'more than ya earned, but don' worry 'bout it. Good luck."

A few despondent days later, I got a call from Orlando, the shirtless carpenter. "Where have you been, dude, we need you." It turns out that the carpentry contractor had been fired, the day after they fired me. The owner of the property—Cal O'Ryan—a physicist at the lab—was taking over the project. He had gotten the names of the carpenters from the contractor before he sent him packing, and apparently knew nothing of my limitations.

Nevertheless, it was back up the hill for me. Someone else had finished the bathtub frame, so I fell in helping the best I could, humping lumber for the other carpenters, rerouting extension cords, retrieving tools dropped from above. At some point, I was working with Pat, who was installing a wood cap on top of a parapet—a continuation of the curved wall that was my earlier downfall.

Pat had divided the half circle into twelve segments, but he couldn't figure out the angle of the joint where the segments met. He tried determining the angle by eye, and cut out the segments. When he set them in place, the last one would not fit.

I started to explain to Pat how to calculate the angle of cut by dividing the number of segments into 360 degrees, and he started getting annoyed.

"Here, dammit," he said, handing me his pencil. Then he began taking the tools out of his apron, handing them to me one by one, and when I could not hold anymore of them, and they started falling to the deck, he took off his hat and threw it down and started to walk away.

I said, "Pat, tomorrow I will bring in a protractor and lay this out for you." I won't bother to write down his reply, but the next day I scribed the angle, and with a little fidgeting figured out the length of the chord.

Pat cut out a new set of caps. All he had to figure out was the length of the pieces that met the main wall of the house. It came out like a piece of fine cabinetry. Cal noticed and gave Pat a compliment on the work that afternoon. From then on, Pat and I were tight.

||

== O ==

||

We worked together through the autumn, and under his tutelage I gained some skill. He had a tender side, too. Once—it was the day before Thanksgiving—I was nailing up blocking inside a closet, using a brand new twenty-two-ounce Estwing. As I began to swing the hammer, its claw hung for a moment on a stud behind me. I remember watching the hammer head, with its razor-sharp waffle pattern sparkling, as it wobbled by on its way to my ring finger—which I had not yet learned to tuck out of the way when holding a nail.

It seemed like the hammerhead just tagged the fingertip, but it tore a nice flap of skin loose.

"Damn," I cried, and dropped my hammer. Pat noticed and went out to his car to get a band-aid. By the time he returned, it was red beneath the fingernail. The pain was excruciating.

Once again, Pat went back to his car, returning with needle nose pliers and a tiny brad. He held the brad with the pliers and heated it with his lighter until the tip started to glow.

"Gimme your hand," he ordered. I gave it to him.

"Now look away."

Then he lightly touched the brad to my fingernail. It penetrated the nail effortlessly. Blood spurted from the little hole, and the pain immediately subsided.

"All set," he said. "Now let's get back to work."

||
== O ==
||

On Christmas Eve, we knocked off early to drink a beer. We got our regular table at Enola Gay's, and Pat launched back into his life in western Massachusetts, weaving his spell on me again, while we drained a couple of pitchers. After a few rounds, the other guys shoved off, but Pat ordered one more pitcher. He poured me a glass, which I barely touched, but as he continued The History of Pat, he finished off the pitcher. Then he suggested that he stop off and wish my girlfriend Merry Christmas. Annamarie and I lived just a few hundred yards off the highway—there's only one that leads back to Santa Fe—so it made sense from a logistical point of view. Still, I protested. Pat replied, "OK, I'll just pop in for a second, and be on my way." Then he gave me that irresistible smile.

"Alright, Pat," I said, "just follow me."

‖
== O ==
‖

I pulled my truck into the driveway, and the Tornado, slinging gravel, swerved in behind me. As Pat lurched out of the car, the bill of his cap hit the doorframe, knocking it sideways across his head. He did not seem to notice. Swaying as he walked, he followed me to the stoop, singing ain't no sunshine when she's gone. Annamarie appeared in the doorway, hands on her hips.

I called up from from the driveway, "Hey Annie, I brought Pat Maloney with me."

"I see. Is he coming in, or is he just going to stand there singing?"

Pat fell silent and stiffened up. He straightened his hat out and hitched up his trousers.

"Pat, come on in. This is Annamarie."

We clambered into the little trailer house. I gave Annamarie a peck on a stony cheek.

Pat greeted her. "Mrs. Addams, how do you do? 'Sa pleasure to meecha." Pat knew we weren't married but called her Mrs. Addams anyway. Annamarie grimaced. She asked him, "Pat, can I fix you a cup of coffee? I was about to have a cup myself."

He cocked his head toward her and raised one eyebrow, and replied, "No, but I'll take a beer if you have one."

I groaned audibly. "Pat, for crissakes..."

At those words, Pat's head sank. The corners of his mouth pulled down, and the twinkle in his eyes vanished. "That's right. Enough is enough."

We sat down, me on the couch, and Pat in a chair on the opposite side, near the door. The little trailer house was so narrow, our knees were almost touching. Annamarie brought in some coffee and sat down next to me, about as far away as the little couch would permit.

So I started telling her about our plans to subcontract the carpentry work for the Grant house. Pat began to beam again. Some force filled his sagging body, and his arms and head became animated again. He rambled on about the plans for the house, how it would be even greater than O'Ryan's. How we would create a partnership, an enduring relationship. How we would create something of value. He repeated those words, "something of value."

Then he talked about how proud his wife, Rosa, was of these prospects. He wanted to introduce me to her.

"I want you to meet Isabella, too." Isabella was his daughter. "Smart girl; she's going to Saint Johns. Beautiful, too. I think you would like her."

30

Annamarie was sitting with her arms folded across her chest and legs crossed. Except for the slow flexing of her elevated foot, she could have been carved out of marble.

But I was in another world, imagining the lovely Isabella. Somewhere in the background, I remember Pat comparing his knockout of a daughter with Annamarie, my Annamarie, who took fierce pride in the severity of her looks; somewhere deep in my suppressed consciousness I knew I should be outraged. But instead, I just sat there, grinning and nodding. Annamarie sat in silence.

Finally, I told him it was time to wind it down, and he got up and went out to his car. Annamarie was still on the couch, still cross-armed and cross-legged, but she had turned her head away, gazing out the south window at the desert beyond.

I started to say something, knowing there was nothing to say. Then I looked out front and noticed that Pat's car had not moved. He had passed out behind the wheel.

So I got up and went outside. Then I opened the driver's side door and shoved him over and drove him back to Santa Fe. Pat rode slumped against the passenger side door, his right arm extended, and his head on his shoulder. The sun was setting, turning the snow on the Sangre De Cristos a salmon color. He lived all the way on the other side of town, somewhere way out Agua Fria. When we arrived at his house, I got out and left him to sleep it off. I glanced at the house and saw two women coming out the door, but I just turned away.

Annamarie had followed us in her truck. I got in, and she drove us back up the highway. By this time, the sun had set, and the moon had made the snow on the mountains luminous. I chattered lamely, pretending it was all in good fun, a few drinks, a crazy old guy, no? Maybe she even believed me, a little bit, anyway.

I don't know how many years it took, after it was all over with her, for me to realize the value of what I'd lost.

Why couldn't I have said to Pat, "Listen up, old man. Annamarie is my woman, and I'm her man. She is beautiful to me, and I don't give a damn what you think."

It was because I was not a man, not then. And perhaps only now.

It Was in the Stars

His truck hauls up a long, wooded slope. When it begins to crest, the new sun strikes the windshield with palpable force. Its light refracts off the dust and spattered insects, dazzling the cab. The blast of sunlight launches him back in time. Could it really have been three years since he met her?

East-bound on the empty highway, he smells something familiar, something comforting. It takes him a moment to recognize the aroma of burning oak. Where he'd lived for the past six years, homes were heated with piñon, its fragrance like incense. On frigid mornings, its smoky haze would dull the colors and soften the lines of the settlements strewn along the Rio Grande and its unreliable tributaries. Now, in the gaining light, he can make out the houses— solitary, and in small groups—and the trees that stand around them: hardwoods, tall and articulated, trees with real leaves.

East. What is it that draws him back? He'd intended to take I-25 up to Denver, to visit some cousins he hadn't seen since he was a kid—but at the last second, he hooked a sharp right onto 84, and then took I-40, east bound. He recalls the Fli-Back he used to play with, smacking the rubber ball with its plywood paddle, harder and harder, trying to snap the elastic cord and launch the ball across the yard, until he'd miss and the ball would come flying back at his face.

Now, coasting down a long hill. The bridge at the bottom is nearly hidden by mist. As he approaches it he makes out the broad, lazy creek. An aluminum row boat, upturned on the bank, reflects a glint of sun. Here are ponds, lakes, rivers. Water—so languid, so undeliberate. Eastward, flying back east.

He is somewhere in Oklahoma, approaching the Arkansas line. Not like that blistering road that runs out toward the Texas panhandle—that westbound stretch he drove almost six years ago, on his way to New Mexico. His plan had been to visit Annamarie, who had moved to El Rancho after their breakup, and then continue to Alaska to work on the pipeline. But he arrived there broke. The Honda shop in Santa Fe hired him on the spot. By the time he had made enough money to move on, he'd patched things up with Annamarie, and was sharing her tiny rented trailer house with her dogs, cats, ferns, and spider plants. Alaska was forgotten.

Now he's heading back east. He had to get out—the cigarette was the last straw. That stale, putrid smell in the bathroom, on top of his mild hangover. If they stopped at two drinks, there was peace; the third drink was war. It could take two more to achieve an armistice.

In fact, the whole blasted thing started with a cigarette, that evening he stopped off in a bar on the outskirts of Sante Fe, on his way home from work. He had a perfectly clear idea how long he could dawdle and how much he could drink before catching hell from Annamarie. But then he noticed a woman, two stools over, slitting open a pack of Newports with a long, cherry red fingernail.

The recollection triggers a craving. First, for a smoke—and then, for the sensation of those painted nails raking his back. It stirs him. She could draw blood, he says to no one—the first sounds he utters in 24 hours.

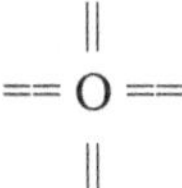

When he pulled into the gravel lot, the sun was still well above the Jemez Mountains—so bright that when he entered the building, he could barely make out the bar. He bumped against a barrel of peanuts next to the door. Beside it was a scoop and a stack of paper bowls, but he just dipped his hat into the barrel and dredged up a full load. Then he selected a stool in the middle of the nearly silent bar.

As his eyes adjusted, he took in the surroundings. The bar itself was a solid slab of ponderosa pine with an unfinished edge. The walls of the building were adobe, and the floor was a chipped and stained concrete slab. Along the front wall was a series rough plywood panels, filling openings that once housed overhead doors. Opposite the entrance, some young men in black jeans and tee shirts were setting up microphones and amplifiers.

People trickled in. Daylight invaded whenever the door opened, and the few people already at the bar and tables—almost all men—would turn to see who arrived. From an alcove at the back came the occasional clatter of billiard balls. A roadie tapped on a mike, and played a clumsy riff on a guitar. Someone at a table hooted at him, and the roadie looked up and stopped playing. Voices and laughter begin to fill the room, echoing off the hard surfaces.

He was already on his second beer, and a pile of empty shells was accumulating on the floor beside his stool. He hadn't noticed when she had walked in, but there she was, an empty stool between them.

With a furtive glance, he took her in. She—Red Nails—was in crisp slacks and a shimmery blouse. Her lipstick matched her nails, and her hair was a brilliant auburn. Almost natural. He wondered if she felt out of place in this raucous, makeshift roadhouse. But then the bartender—a huge bearlike man— leaned over the bar to receive her dainty kiss on his hairy cheek. No, she was a regular.

In a moment, she was joined by another man and woman, who sat on either side of her. She greeted the couple, and they began to chatter. Sitting closest to him was the man, wearing a sun bleached Carhartt jacket and Levis, threadbare at the knees. The other woman, her hair in thick braids, wore a white peasant blouse and nothing under it. Her flowered skirt draped over the tops of her wellingtons. The two women began an animated conversation, seemingly ignoring the man between them. Silently, he drained his mug, and was about to call for the check when Red Nails fished an unopened pack of cigarettes from her purse.

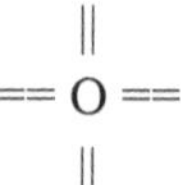

The sun is high now. Billboards advertise restaurants; a sensation flows up from his gut. Yesterday, he withdrew a hundred and twenty dollars from the account, leaving her enough for the payment on the trailer house and some groceries until she got her next check. He scraped up nearly twenty more in loose bills and change. But fifty dollars was already shot on gas, and three more on dinner in Amarillo. A so-called burrito—what Texans have the nerve to call chili is pathetic. In his head he runs through the numbers, a thousand more miles, seventy more for gas. If he spends another night in the cab, he can afford breakfast.

While he makes those calculations, a promising exit at Morrilton sails past. He nearly misses the next one, but at the last second, he swerves onto the road to Plumerville. The duffle in the passenger seat tumbles into his shoulder, and the surprise sends him across the center line. A horn blares, and he yanks the truck back into its lane. He can't be that tired—after all, he and that woman—what was her name—had once driven to the coast in fifty-two hours. Crazy Sue, that's it. Collins' wife. Doing ninety most of the way, in that beat up VW. When they arrived in Santa Barbara, he noticed the tire treads were worn to the cords. That's when he realized just how crazy she really was.

Now, Sweeney's Family Diner appears on the right. There are only two cars in the lot—a jacked up Trans Am, and another marked Conway County Sheriff. He pulls in anyway, right beside the bubble-topped sedan. Some of his bigger tools didn't fit in the crossover box, and lay loose in the bed, so maybe the proximity to the law might give a thief a moment's pause.

He takes a table by the front window, so he can keep an eye on the truck. In his reflection in the glass, he notices how wild his hair and beard have become. Two men in tan uniforms are straddling stools at the counter. The projecting butts of their service revolvers remind him of the shotgun lying in his rifle rack. It's legal in New Mexico—but in Arkansas? Too late anyway, too late to get up and just leave, without attracting attention.

"Coffee?" The waitress startles him.

"Yes, Ma'am. And two eggs, sunny side, please."

"Breakfast is over at ten."

"Sorry, I didn't realize how late it is."

The two officers look over their shoulders and take a moment before turning back around to their plates. Across the room, an enormous man in a black Stetson looks up, fork frozen before an open mouth.

She says, "I got a hamburger, a cheeseburger, a BLT, and a catfish po boy. They all come with fries."

Again, he thinks about excusing himself and getting back on his way, but the aroma of frying grease causes him to reconsider. "Thank you, I'll have the catfish," he replies.

As soon as the waitress leaves, he walks as calmly as he can to the restroom. When he returns, a mug of tepid coffee is at his place.

She would have walked out, without so much as a thanks anyway or an excuse me. It seemed she was always looking for something to be slighted or insulted by—a chance to fight, to fight back. It was a trap he'd always fall into, swallowing the bait, and then his blood was up, too, and there was no stopping until it got ugly.

||
== O ==
||

But that evening at the Santa Fe roadhouse, those smiling eyes, that natural laugh, arrested him. How carefully she removed the cellophane, picked open the foil, and rapped the pack against the heel of her thumb three times to produce some filters; how she neatly extracted the proudest one with her painted lips. All so perfectly unconscious, never missing a beat of her conversation.

He groped in his pocket for a match, but she—not noticing—had already thumbed open a Zippo and struck a flame. As she tilted her chin up to apply the fire, she gave her head a shake that tousled the waves of copper over her shoulders.

The bartender gestured toward his empty mug; he replied with a nod. A strum on an electric guitar hushed the room. Heads turned toward the sound. The man between them got up and headed for the rest room. She drew on her cigarette and exhaled. As the band tuned up and started their patter, he gazed at her profile in the mirror behind the bar.

The smoke drifted back past him; the odor stimulated a sensation that ran up the inside of his arms. As she turned back to use the ashtray, her eyes met his in the mirror. She did not smile or look away, until he lowered his eyes. Then she swiveled her stool directly at him.

"Is there something you want?" she asked.

She glanced down at the hat still half full of peanuts. At first it looked like she was smiling, but he could see her jaw muscle tensing and releasing.

"I'm sorry for staring," he said.

"It's nothing. No offense taken." He searched her eyes for assurance but could find none. She took another drag and started to turn away.

Then he said, "You know, there is something I'd like—I mean, if you don't mind me asking."

She turned back languidly. "Oh, and what is that?"

"This is going to sound dumb—"

"Just spit it out."

"Well, even though I pretty much quit smoking, I still enjoy it once in a while. But if I buy a pack, then I start smoking again like crazy. So, if you give me one of yours, I'd buy you a whole new pack."

"Is that all you want—a cigarette?"

He nodded. Her stony aspect dissolved, and she issued a surprisingly loud laugh from deep in her chest. The woman sitting next to her tried to gain a view of the discussion. She, Red Nails, grabbed the pack from the bar and reached across the empty stool to offer him one. He held up his hand.

"No, wait, let me get another pack for you first—there's got to be a machine here somewhere."

"Never mind that, I got plenty. But you could buy me another drink."

As she began to move to the closer stool, the other man returned, headed for the same seat. She shifted to stand in front of him, blocking him from the stool. She was nearly as tall as him—and he was every bit of six feet. Confused, he stopped before them.

"George," she said, "This man is in need of a cigarette, and I offered to help him out."

George snapped back to the two of them, "Rose is all about charity—and temperance, and chastity. Right, Rosie?"

"Right, you smart ass. You just got the order backwards. So why don't you be charitable and go sit down?" George shook his head and complied. Then she slipped onto the closer stool and bumped her shoulder against his like they were old buddies. "Now, where were we?" she said. "Yes, you're going to buy me a seven and seven. And I must pay the price."

He summoned the bartender and ordered her drink. Surprised that his own mug was already empty, he ordered another beer for himself. Then, Red

Nails—Rose—gave him a cigarette. As she lit it for him, he noticed some engraving on the lighter.

"Thank you," he said. "What's that marking on the lighter? Can I see it?"

She passed him the lighter. On one side was the image of a prancing animal with curling horns. On the obverse was the Marine Corps emblem, and the words:

SEMPER FI
JASON

"My little brother gave it to me, after he came home from Vietnam," she says.

"I hope he made it back home in one piece."

"I'm not too sure he did. He won't talk about it. He's a teacher now, second and third graders. Can you believe that?"

"I guess so, why not?" He turned the lighter back around. "What's with the goat?"

She laughed that deep laugh again. "It's a ram, dummy. He's an Aries. Get it?"

"No, what do you mean?"

"Aries, god of war. Aries is ruled by Mars, and he's a warrior. A Marine."

"Give me a break. You don't really believe in that stuff, do you?"

"Maybe I do, and maybe I don't. But wouldn't you like to believe that there was something that explains who we are? Some way to figure out who we should be with?"

"Well, sure, but I don't believe that some planet or star has any influence over us. What about your upbringing, your mother, your father?"

"If you had a father like we did, you wouldn't want to be under his influence. You'd be glad for some stars, if he was your old man. Bastard had big hands, and he liked to use them. On all of us—even my mother."

They both fell silent for a moment. The bartender delivered their drinks. Then she said, "Forget it. So anyway, what's your sign?" She took a sip of her drink and licked her lips.

"Geezus," he said, his voice trailing off. He shook his head.

"Out with it," she demanded.

He sighed. "I'm not really sure. It's either Leo or Virgo. I'm sort of in between."

"What's your birthday?"

"August 22."

37

"Of course—you're right on the cusp." Then her eyes widened, and she gasped, "Oh my god! My birthday is December 22. I'm on the cusp between Sagittarius and Capricorn. We're in perfect trine!"

"What in heaven and earth does that mean?"

"It means you're coming home with me, honey. I'll explain it all to you later."

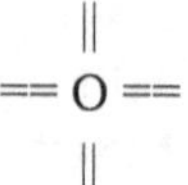

He struggles to keep his eyelids apart, as darkness begins to hide the rolling hills, farms, and wooded valleys. Now, however, the exits are more frequent, and the lights and billboards of yet another city—Knoxville—compel him to continue, far enough beyond their glow, to find another rest stop or deserted side road, somewhere he can pull over and catch a few hours of sleep.

What if? What if he had paid his tab and gone back to El Rancho instead? To Annamarie, to her makeshift household, the mattress on the floor, the bookshelves of drooping 1x10's stacked on concrete blocks. To her disdain—for his smoking and his diet, for the dirt and grease impacted in his knuckles, for his fumbling calloused hands. Yet also, to her willingness—to accept him every night, no matter how dull and routine it had become. To accept his mediocrity, his absence of ambition. To the opportunity she offered him for his own redemption.

No, he traded it all for this, that one night, that one night that should have been no more than one night, if it ever should have been at all. The headlights part the darkness like the prow of a ship, leaving behind a wake of shadows, as the truck continues, rolling, plunging, surging—eastward.

photo National Fish and Wildlife Service

Evening In Los Luceros

Like clockwork, a little after sundown, Rosa raises her
snout from her front paws. It's that damn skunk again.
She whines and snivels, and parades back and forth
until you have to open the door. You pray that
she won't find it, but you know she will. And,
by the way, tomato juice does not work. Later, after
you're between the sheets, you hear the first howl.
Usually it starts up the valley, and progresses
downstream as the conversation is taken up by other
coyotes, and probably some dogs as well. I've seen
feral dogs, too, back in the barrancas, perhaps abandoned
as puppies, so skinny they could hardly stand.

At last the coyotes are silent—silent as the shooting stars.
You don't need to hear them to know they're there.